D1081211

GECKO PRESS

When we were alone in the world

Also by Ulf Nilsson and Eva Eriksson
All the Dear Little Animals (Gecko Press, 2006)

This edition first published in Australia and New Zealand in 2009 by Gecko Press
PO Box 9335, Marion Square, Wellington 6141, New Zealand
info@geckopress.com

First published by Bonnier Carlsen Bokförlag, Stockholm, Sweden
Published in the English language by arrangement with Bonnier Group Agency,
Stockholm, Sweden

National Library of New Zealand Cataloguing-in-Publication Data
Nilsson, Ulf, 1948-
När vi var ensamma i världen. English.
When we were alone in the world / written by Ulf Nilsson and
illustrated by Eva Eriksson.
ISBN 978-1-87746-735-6 (hbk.)—978-1-87746-734-9 (pbk.)
[1. Brothers—Fiction.] I. Eriksson, Eva. II. Title.
839.7374—dc 22

Edited by Penelope Todd
Typeset by Archetype, New Zealand
Printed by Proost, Belgium

For more curiously good books, visit www.geckopress.com

When we were alone in the world

Ulf Nilsson and Eva Eriksson

GECKO PRESS

Οne day at school I learned to tell the time. Nine o'clock, ten o'clock, one o'clock, two o'clock.

At three o'clock Dad usually came to get me. But he wasn't outside. In the end I went home by myself. Our house is just down the road. But why hadn't he come? What had happened?

The door to the house was locked. I called out to Mum and
Dad, but they weren't there. They were gone, and so was my
little brother.

 I worked out that they were dead. Something must have
happened. Probably they'd been run over by a truck.

I sat on the steps and cried. It was very sad. I wasn't even six years old and I was all alone in the world. And the house where we lived was locked. Alone in the world.

What had happened to my little brother?

Maybe he was at playschool when Mum and Dad got run over by the truck?

I ran the whole way there. It's not very far. I saw him in the sandpit, pouring sand over a little girl with a dummy in her mouth.

I hugged him and cried. He looked at me in surprise.

I had to stop crying at once. I couldn't show him how terrible things were. That would make him sad.

'It's just you and me now,' I said, 'alone in the world. But I'll look after you very, very well. Everything will be just like normal.'

The teacher was chasing after a girl climbing the fence. I took my little brother by the hand and we sneaked away. We were on our way home.

Everything would be just the same! When he came home from playschool, my little brother liked to watch TV for a bit. Usually he sat on the mat, eating a little biscuit.

That was a big problem. We had no house. We had no mat. We had no TV. We had no beds to sleep in.

And above all, we had no little biscuit.

But I had promised to look after him!

And I would.

First we'd build a house! I found a long stick amongst the
bushes. It was no good for a house. But it could be a flagpole.
   'First we'll make a flagpole!'

I tied my hankie to the top and poked the flagpole into the ground. Very good. We would manage without Mum and Dad …

Mum and Dad! It made me sad to think about them. My eyes filled with tears. But I couldn't cry in front of my little brother. And anyway my hankie was up the top of the pole. I got angry instead, thinking about the truck that ran them over.

We went round the garden looking for something to build a
house with. It would be a beautiful little house, and we could
live there till we grew old, left home and went to university.

My little brother found some rotten sticks. But I was lucky
and I found five white planks that Dad planned to use to make a
new fence. They were under a tarpaulin.

We poor children had no nails and no hammer. But we banged the planks a little way into the grass with a stone. They were a bit wobbly.

Then we put planks on the roof as well. That helped make the house a bit stronger.

It was a very beautiful little white house. With a flagpole. On a lawn. I was proud.

I didn't know if we would be able to live in it when we grew up. But we could build on eventually. We had more planks.

Inside the house I made two beds from branches and moss.
We brought in lots of old leaves which can go on top of you
when you're asleep.

'A leaf blanket is very nice and warm,' I said.

I covered my little brother so he lay under a big pile of leaves.
His little eyes peeped out at me. He blinked.

He said he wanted to watch TV.

It's quite hard to make a TV.

I started with an old carton I found in the rubbish heap.

I ripped out a hole where the picture would be. I made a remote control from a smaller box. I had a pen in my backpack and I drew on the buttons.

My little brother's rotten stick went on the top for an antenna, just like our neighbour's one.

I pushed the button on the remote. Nothing happened.

'The batteries are dead. Anyway there's nothing good on TV these days,' I said, looking at the screen.

I sounded just like Dad and I rubbed my chin just like he did.

My little brother said he would like a biscuit before he watched TV. Or some cake. Or butter.

He was trying to trick me. I knew very well he wasn't allowed to eat just butter. But we brothers had to stick together now, so I didn't say anything.

I pulled up some carrots from the vegetable garden, but he didn't think much of them.

Then I remembered we could borrow things from our
neighbour. Sometimes when you run out of something in the
kitchen, you go over to the neighbour's and you borrow it.

We knocked on our neighbour's door. He was an old man
with a moustache and a checked vest.

'Can we borrow some eggs?' I asked.

He went to the kitchen.

'Three eggs,' I called. 'And you could break them.'

He found a bowl for the eggs.

'And a cup of sugar.'

He rummaged in his pantry.

I had learned how to make a cake. What else did you need?

'And a little butter. And some flour and a teaspoon of vanilla sugar.'

The old man came back with the bowl. Everything was there.

'Butter!!!' my little brother said happily.

We mixed everything together using the antenna.

It was a beautiful cake mix. But I couldn't think how to make it into a cake. How can you do that without an oven?

My little brother thought the cake mix was good as it was. He ate it with his hands, straight from the bowl.

In the meantime I made my own TV programme. There was a little penguin.

'Pingu, Pingu,' I sang, hopping round inside the box.

My little brother was pleased. He laughed so hard that he bounced and shook. He had cake mix on both hands and in his hair.

'Pingu, Pingu,' I sang.

He was so happy because he still knew nothing. One day when he was bigger, I would tell him the whole sad story.

'Well, my dear little brother, once upon a time we had some parents, but ...'

The wind blew through the gaps in the rickety walls. It was such a shame about us.

I started to cry.

'Pingu sad,' said my little brother.

And I explained that Pingu was sad because his mother and father had been run over by a terrible red truck which came sliding over the ice. Then Pingu and his little sister couldn't get inside the igloo. They sat outside, freezing.

Pingu cried harder and louder.

'Other one,' said my little brother.

He wanted something different on TV. Me too.

Then someone looked in through a gap in the wall.

It was Dad.

'My oh my! We've been so worried! They rang us from playschool …'

Someone lifted planks off the roof.

It was Mum.

'We came from work as fast as we could!'

Then they took us in their arms and
carried us inside.

The little house fell over by itself.

I didn't understand a thing.

'What about the truck then?' I asked.

'What truck?' said my mother.

They gave us sandwiches, but my little brother was too full to eat anything. We watched some TV. It was a funny programme.

'What did you do at school?' asked my mother. 'And why did you go home early?'

'I learned to tell the time,' I said. 'Nine o'clock, ten o'clock, one o'clock, two o'clock.'

Mum showed me her watch.

'Nine o'clock, ten o'clock, *eleven o'clock, twelve o'clock,* one o'clock, two o'clock.'

Dad said: 'The teacher rang and said you'd gone home two hours early.'

'Oh,' I said.

Mum's eyes filled with tears. 'Now I understand! You thought we were gone …'

Mum and Dad tried to hug us. But me and my little brother were busy watching TV. We laughed.

I ate my sandwich.

My little brother burped.